Greetings from

SANDY BEACH

Copyright © Blackbird Design Pty Ltd 1990
First published 1990 by Thomas C. Lothian Pty Ltd,
Melbourne, Australia

This edition first published 1997 by
Happy Cat Books, Bradfield, Essex CO11 2UT

Reprinted 1999

A CIP catalogue record for this book is available from
the British Library

ISBN 1 899248 41 2

Printed in Hong Kong

Greetings from
SANDY
BEACH

Bob Graham

Happy Cat Books

There were plenty of tears at the start of
our holiday.
Dad cried about leaving our dog.
Mum cried about leaving Grandma and Grandad.

Gerald cried because he'd been awake all night,
(over-excited and couldn't sleep).
I cried because everyone else was crying.
And we were only going for two days!

It was better when we got going.
Dad dabbed at his nose for a while
with wet paper tissues.

Mum started on the toffees
before we even left our street.

Gerald went straight to sleep
with his mouth open.

And I put my headphones on
and listened to my tape.
(The Best of the Heartbeats.)

The trip took forever. Nothing much happened
on the way.
Except a girl in a bus stuck her tongue out at me.

Mum and Dad sang songs I didn't know—
And Gerald threw up.

At the campsite things picked up. There were
people on motorbikes. They were called
The Disciples of Death.
Dad didn't like the look of them.

'Don't go near them,' said my Dad.
'Stay away from them Gerald,' said my Mum.

They had a dog with goggles that rode up
on the petrol tank.
It was the best thing I ever saw in my life.

Then the kids in the bus arrived.
'Must be some kind of school outing,' my Dad said.
My Mum was walking around with
toffee papers stuck on her seat.

Gerald sat in the sand playing with his plastic
charging rhino.
And that girl stuck her tongue out at me again.
Then we put the tent up.

At least we *tried* to put the tent up.

Dad couldn't figure it out . . .
Although Mum got her bit up.

I looked after Gerald who kept wandering off.

The Disciples finally showed us how.
Dad looked nervous and smiled at them a lot.

We didn't go straight into the water.
Dad wanted to enjoy the sun.
'We've got the beach to ourselves,' he said.

'It's so peaceful here,' my Mum kept saying.
Gerald was happy enough. Just blobbing
around in the sand.

The girl from the bus fell right out of the sky
onto Dad. He wasn't too pleased. 'You've got the
whole beach,' he said, 'and you land on me.'

So we shared the beach with the school kids.
They played a 'Cowboys Getting Shot' game,
to see how far they could roll.

I joined in.

It was just like the cowboys in the films.

High dives from the tops of buildings,

into the dusty street.

I won.
The Girl with The Tongue was quite impressed.
So were The Disciples of Death.

We shared the water with the school kids too.
Dad washed off the sand, the sand that had
fallen out of the sky and stuck to his sunburn oil.

Mum played puddles with Gerald. I stood away
from them a bit. I am embarrassed by my
parents when other kids are around.
I don't know why.

The school kids went back for lunch, with their teachers. (Fancy seeing your teacher in just a pair of flowery shorts.)

Dad and I made a mermaid.

Mum wrote Gerald's name in the sand.
Not with a stick . . . with Gerald!

We camped that night in the tent.
Dad cooked the dinner—Camp Stew out of a tin.
Mum and Dad played word games
with little wooden squares.

There was a lot of shrieking from the
school camp.
Gerald went straight to sleep (very pink
from the sun).
So did I.

Next day we played boats in the rock pool,
with some ice-cream sticks from
The Disciples.

We buried Mum in the sand.

Dad caught a rather small fish,
and Gerald ate something disgusting
from his fishing basket.

And we slept our second night in the tent.

In the morning we all packed up.
The Lady Disciple bought us a
raspberry Icy Pop each.

The Tongue Girl gave me a souvenir shell
with the name of the camping park on it.
And the biggest bikie sat Gerald right up
on the petrol tank.

They all passed us on the way home.
First the bus, then The Disciples with their
little white dog, his ears streaming in the wind.

'They were all right really,' said my Dad.
'Once you got to know them,' he added, a bit
further down the road.

There was still a slight smell of old fish
about Gerald. Dad held him at arm's length.
'Let's get Gerald into the bath,' my Mum said.

It was quite a while back now. But I've still got the Icy Pop sticks and the shell.

Souvenirs I guess.